Finn and the Dentist

by Jill Atkins and Valentina Bandera

W
FRANKLIN WATTS
LONDON•SYDNEY

Dad helped Oliver and Finn brush their teeth.

"My tooth is wobbly," said Oliver.

He showed Dad his wobbly tooth.

"We must go to the dentist,"
Dad said.

"She will look at your teeth."

"I like the dentist," said Oliver.
"You sit in a big chair
and she tickles your teeth.
Then she checks them."

"I don't like the dentist," said Finn.
Dad laughed. "You have never
been to the dentist," he said.

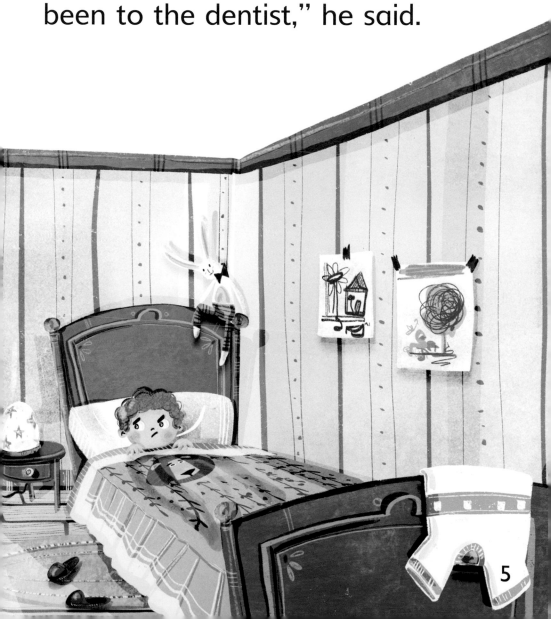

After breakfast the next day,

Dad got the coats.

"We are going to see the dentist,"

he said.

Oliver held Finn's hand
and they set off.

They went into the waiting room.

The lady smiled at Finn.

"Have you been to the dentist before?" she said.

"No," said Finn.

They went into the dentist's room.

"Look at my chair," said the dentist.

"It can go up and down."

Oliver went up and down

in the chair.

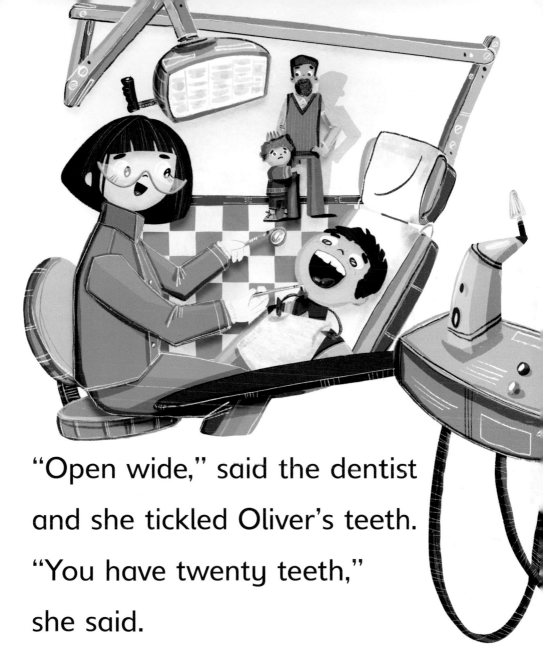

"Open wide," said the dentist
and she tickled Oliver's teeth.
"You have twenty teeth,"
she said.
"They look nice and clean."

"My tooth is wobbly," said Oliver.

"It will come out soon,"
said the dentist.

"And a new tooth will grow."

The dentist looked at Finn.
"Come and sit in my chair,"
she said.

Finn went up and down
in the chair.

He let the dentist tickle his teeth.

He let her count them.

"You have sixteen teeth,"
she said.

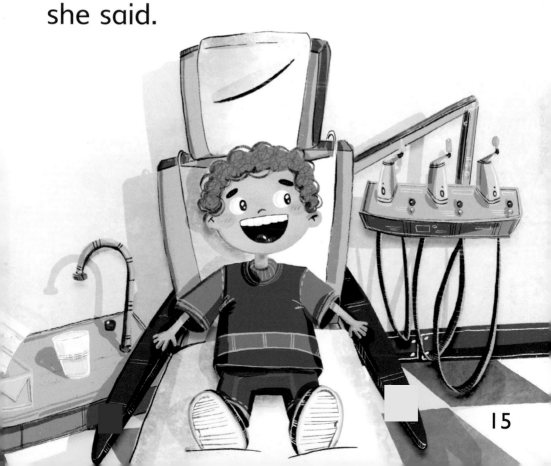

"Your teeth are nice and clean,"
the dentist said.
"Yes," said Finn. "Oliver and I clean
our teeth in the morning
and when we go to bed."

"Fantastic!" said the dentist.

"Here are some stickers.

One for Oliver and one for Finn."

"Thank you," they said.

"I like the dentist," said Finn.

"Can we come again tomorrow?"

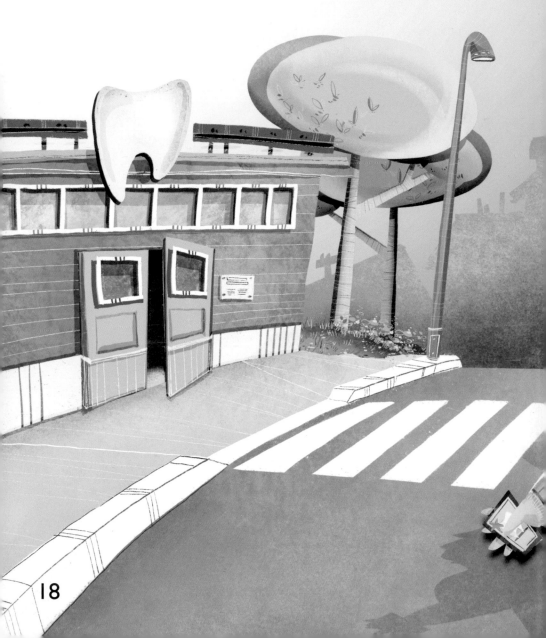

Story trail

Start

Start at the beginning of the story trail. Ask your child to retell the story in their own words, pointing to each picture in turn to recall the sequence of events.

Independent Reading

This series is designed to provide an opportunity for your child to read on their own. These notes are written for you to help your child choose a book and to read it independently.

In school, your child's teacher will often be using reading books which have been banded to support the process of learning to read. Use the book band colour your child is reading in school to help you make a good choice. *Finn and the Dentist* is a good choice for children reading at Green Band in their classroom to read independently.

The aim of independent reading is to read this book with ease, so that your child enjoys the story and relates it to their own experiences.

About the book

It is Finn's first time visiting the dentist and he is not keen. His brother Oliver helps him with his nerves, and Finn ends up enjoying it so much, he wants to come again!

Before reading

Help your child to learn how to make good choices by asking: "Why did you choose this book? Why do you think you will enjoy it?" Look at the cover together and ask: "What do you think the story will be about?" Support your child to think of what they already know about the story context. Read the title aloud and ask: "Do you think that Finn will enjoy going to see the dentist?"

Remind your child that they can try to sound out the letters to make a word if they get stuck.

Decide together whether your child will read the story independently or read it aloud to you.

During reading

If reading aloud, support your child if they hesitate or ask for help by telling the word. Remind your child of what they know and what they can do independently.

If reading to themselves, remind your child that they can come and ask for your help if stuck.

After reading

Support comprehension by asking your child to tell you about the story. Use the story trail to encourage your child to retell the story in the right sequence, in their own words.

Help your child think about the messages in the book that go beyond the story and ask: "Do you think that Oliver helped Finn when he was worried about going to see the dentist? Why/why not?"

Give your child a chance to respond to the story: "Did you have a favourite part? Have you been to visit the dentist? Have you ever helped someone feel less worried about doing something?"

Extending learning

Help your child understand the story structure by using the same story context and adding different elements. "Let's make up a new story about Oliver helping Finn do or try something he is nervous about. What will this thing be? How might Oliver help?"

In the classroom, your child's teacher may be teaching polysyllabic words (words with more than one syllable). There are many in this book that you could look at with your child, for example:

wobb/ly, den/tist, tick/les, twen/ty, six/teen, morn/ing, stick/er, fan/tas/tic.

Franklin Watts
First published in Great Britain in 2020
by The Watts Publishing Group

Series Editors: Jackie Hamley and Melanie Palmer
Series Advisors: Dr Sue Bodman and Glen Franklin
Series Designer: Peter Scoulding

A CIP catalogue record for this book is
available from the British Library.

ISBN 978 1 4451 7070 1 (hbk)
ISBN 978 1 4451 7072 5 (pbk)
ISBN 978 1 4451 7071 8 (library ebook)

Printed in China

Franklin Watts
An imprint of
Hachette Children's Group
Part of The Watts Publishing Group
Carmelite House
50 Victoria Embankment
London EC4Y 0DZ

An Hachette UK Company
www.hachette.co.uk

www.franklinwatts.co.uk